DOODLEBUG

Also by
IRENE BRADY

America's Horses and Ponies
Beaver Year
A Mouse Named Mus
Owlet, the Great Horned Owl

DOODLEBUG

Written and illustrated by
IRENE BRADY

Houghton Mifflin Company Boston 1977

For Larry

Library of Congress Cataloging in Publication Data

Brady, Irene.
  Doodlebug.

  SUMMARY: A young girl finds that the injured, disheveled pony she buys out of pity at an auction is really the black stallion of her dreams.
  1. Ponies—Legends and stories. [1. Ponies—Fiction] I. Title.
PZ10.3.B728Do   [Fic]   77-4168
ISBN 0-395-25782-4

Jennifer Dickens wrinkled her nose and peered around from her high perch on the top bar of the pole corral. Just below her stood a skinny, shaggy black pony with a lame forefoot. The corrals and chutes behind the livestock auction barns were empty in the warm spring sunshine. She'd waited the whole winter for this auction, and all for nothing. Not one horse had been brought to be sold. Only that one little pony.

Kicking the poles angrily, Jennifer glared down.

"Dirty dumb pony!" she muttered. The pony looked up at her, then it limped closer and reached up to nibble her sneaker. Only then did Jennifer see the dried blood on his foreleg, and the angry look on her face changed to concern. Poor pony! Surely someone would buy him today and doctor his leg! She scratched between the pony's ears with her sneaker.

Jennifer loved horses. All horses, really. But the horse she wanted was a Beautiful Black Stallion with Flowing Mane and Tail (she always thought about it in capital letters). And it just *had* to be more beautiful then Myra Banks's chestnut mare, Daisy!

She swung her legs over the top pole and dropped to the dusty ground outside the pen. Pulling a long brown braid moodily, she reached through the bars and scratched under the shabby pony's forelock. There wasn't any use dreaming. All she had was fourteen dollars and fifty-two cents, and that wouldn't buy a real horse. Her folks didn't have enough to help her, and she had done everything she could think of to make money herself. All last summer she had weeded and picked strawberries in her garden and sold them to the Farmer's Market. She had taken care of Mr. Kistler's chickens when he had to be gone for a week. She had saved every penny in her Beautiful Black Stallion Savings Jar. But how much black stallion could you buy with fourteen dollars and fifty-two cents, honestly now? Jennifer sighed . . . One hoof, maybe.

She turned and walked gloomily into the auction barn, her fingers wrapped tightly around the dollar bills in her pants pocket.

Just inside the big barn she stopped and looked up at the crowded rows of seats for her mom and dad, who had come to buy some dairy goats for their farm. They must have left, she decided, for the last of the goats had been auctioned off a few minutes ago. She was just about to push through the crowd along the arena fence and leave the barn when she heard the auctioneer start up his chatter again.

Jennifer loved to hear the auctioneer's nonsense words, even though half the time she couldn't understand them. She stopped to listen. The black pony had been pushed, stumbling, into the ring and the auctioneer was trying to sell him.

"Who'll gimmee twenny-fie dollahs for this fine ani-mule?" he laughed noisily over the loudspeaker.

"Twenny, twenny-fie, ah-gimmee twenny, gimmee twenny-fie," he rattled on, but nobody seemed interested until a fat man with a mole on his chin raised his hand and yelled, "Give ya a buck-fifty!" Jennifer gasped. That fat man was the butcher! She had heard about butchers who sold horsemeat in their shops. Jennifer felt sick with horror.

Just then the pony saw Jennifer and slowly limped to where she stood against the arena fence. He nickered softly and Jennifer grew weak all over. Horsemeat.

Suddenly a determined look crossed over her face.

"Two dollars!" she shouted defiantly. Her heart beat loudly and her hands turned clammy as five hundred people and the auctioneer peered at her in surprise.

"I have the money," she cried, and pulled the handful of dollar bills from her pocket to wave at the auctioneer. She gripped the pony's mane tightly. The butcher wouldn't get *this* little pony! The auctioneer grinned. Maybe he'd be able to sell the injured pony after all. Sometimes no one would even make an offer for a lame animal.

So the bidding went on, Jennifer shouting one dollar more than the butcher each time. A few confused minutes later, she suddenly owned one skinny, dirty, shaggy, lame black pony, two quarters and two pennies. And that's all. She had spent a whole year's savings on the ugly little pony.

Taking a deep breath, Jennifer crawled through the fence and looped her belt around the pony's neck. There were tears in her eyes as she thought about the Black Stallion with Flowing Mane and Tail, but her hands were gentle as she led the lame pony from the arena.

Jennifer's mom and dad were very surprised to see her towing a limping pony toward the pickup truck where they waited with three bleating goats.

"Good grief, Jenny!" her dad burst out. "What do you expect to do with THAT wreck?" Then he saw the tears in her eyes and both he and her mom listened sympathetically while she explained about the butcher.

"Well," sighed her mom, "I guess we can get them all in the truck." She shook her head. "How do you plan to feed him, Jenny?" The Dickens' farm was a small one and every animal had to pay its own way. Jennifer knew that.

"Maybe I could take care of all the goats to earn his feed," she whispered. Dad pursed his lips and looked thoughtful. "We'll think of something. Now let's get this livestock home. We have a lot to do before it gets dark."

Dad and Mom had to lift while Jennifer pulled on the belt to boost the pony into the truck. Then the goats easily jumped up beside him and Dad snubbed each one to a corner post. Jennifer was to ride in the back and

steady the pony. Dad put up the rear gate on the pickup and off they went down the bumpy road toward the farm.

The ride was hard on the pony. Whenever the truck hit a bump, the goats lurched against the pony's injured leg. Jennifer tried to hold him tight against the pickup but it didn't always help. It was an awful ride, made even worse by seeing Myra Banks, who lived near the Dickens' house, cantering along the road on beautiful Daisy. Myra was always bragging about Daisy. Jennifer looked at her own new pony and almost cried. He was *so* ugly!

They finally reached the farm. Dad and Mom helped her walk the pony down a long board braced against the pickup bed. Jennifer spread straw knee-deep in an empty stall in the old barn for him.

When the pony felt the soft straw under him, he gave a deep sigh and lay down with relief. Then they took a good look at his leg.

"It's pretty bad," Jennifer's father shook his head. "It looks like a nasty cut and a sprain. Someone has mistreated this pony." Jennifer's father had once worked for a veterinarian, so he knew just what to do. He got some scissors, warm water, soap, and ointment from the house and they cleaned away the hair and dried blood. Jennifer held the pony's head and gently scratched the dirty mane and face. She knew it took a lot of courage on his part not to kick out or try to bite. She smoothed his mane, then she happened to look into his ear. Wonder grew on her face as she bent closer for a better look. There, tattooed deep in his shaggy ear, was a long number and the name DOODLEBUG!

"Doodlebug?" she said softly. The pony jerked his head up and looked at her with deep brown eyes. That must be his name, all right!

She showed the tattoo to her parents. "Somebody

must have valued this pony once, to have gone to all the trouble of tattooing," exclaimed her mother. "I wonder what stories this pony could tell us."

Jennifer wondered too. Suddenly the pony seemed more than just a dirty castoff. She looked at him with new respect.

At last they were finished with the doctoring.

"It probably won't ever heal perfectly, Jenny," her dad told her honestly. "He'll probably always have a little bit of a limp. But if you soak it maybe twice every day it will get a lot better."

And so she did. Every morning before school, Jennifer fed and brushed Doodlebug and soaked his foot in a bucket of hot salt water. Then she rushed to feed the goats to help earn the pony's hay and grain. Every night after school she did all those things over again, then took Doodlebug for a walk. Soon he was able to trot with only a slight limp, and with the constant brushing, good care, and warm spring days, he began to lose his matted winter coat. It was then that Jennifer realized that Doodlebug was much better looking than she had thought. His summer coat was sleek and short and shiny from her brushing. The shaggy hair had hidden a long slender body without the usual pony potbelly. His head was trim and proud, with big nostrils. His legs were slim and clean. And when he trotted! Jennifer could hardly believe how he picked up his feet and almost danced as he trotted. The only sign of his injury was a slight hesitation as he put that foot down. It was marvelous!

When summer came, Jennifer spent many hours sitting beside Doodlebug in the pasture. One evening she was talking to him as she often did.

"You know, Doodlebug, now that you're well, it's time for you to earn your keep. I'll ride you every day and we'll make some saddlebags so you can help me carry strawberries to the Farmer's Market." She snapped a rein to his halter, stroking him softly, then she slid lightly up onto his back. Doodlebug seemed astonished. He snorted and rolled his eyes, so that she was sure he had never been ridden before.

Jennifer was a good rider — she had swallowed her pride many times and begged Myra for rides on Daisy. Now she lay low over Doodlebug's neck while he pranced and trotted nervously across the pasture, looking over his shoulders constantly. But it was a dreadful ride, rough and bouncy. Jennifer could hardly hang on. Doodlebug's beautiful high-flying trot knocked

all the breath out of her. Myra's Daisy didn't trot like
that at all! Jennifer slid off in dismay, her bones aching.
What good was a pony if you couldn't ride him? She
patted him and praised him. It was no good to scold him
about something he couldn't help. But her heart was
heavy. "Oh Doodlebug," she groaned, "what on earth
are you good for?"

A few days later Jennifer's mother came out to
where Jennifer was brushing Doodlebug in the pasture.

"Jennifer," she began, "have you thought of something your pony can do to earn his feed?" Jennifer shook her head sadly. She knew her parents thought Doodlebug was worthless.

"If you aren't going to ride him, maybe he could pull a wagon."

"A wagon?" asked Jennifer with a frown.

"Yes, we need someone to deliver the goat milk every day over the hill to the Johnsons and the Browns. Your dad will make a cart and harness if you're willing to do the job. You could take your strawberries to market in the cart, too," she added.

Jennifer looked out across the pasture and thought about Myra galloping past on beautiful Daisy. She looked back at her little pony. All Doodlebug ever did was eat. It was embarrassing. Maybe he could at least pull a cart with style, she thought glumly.

"Yeah, Mom," she sighed. "I guess we can do that okay." Her hand, which had been resting on Doodlebug's sleek back, dropped limply to her side. A cart horse! How awful! She'd never be able to look Myra in the face again! Two big tears gathered in her eyes and she blinked fiercely to keep them in. Neither her mother nor her pony would ever guess how she felt about Doodlebug pulling a cart!

Jennifer's dad made the cart as beautiful as he could, using bike tires and painting it grass-green with yellow trim. But Jennifer hated the very sight of it.

Carefully following instructions from a library book, Jennifer began to teach Doodlebug how to be a carthorse. But it was funny how the black pony seemed

to know more about it than Jennifer did. Very soon, it seemed that he was ready to pull the cart.

She winced the first time she slipped the freshly oiled leather harness straps over Doodlebug's back and fastened them to the cart shafts. Doodlebug, tied to the corral fence, quivered with excitement when the straps touched him, and Jennifer looked at him with worry in her eyes. Would he kick the cart or try to run? She climbed cautiously into the little cart and loosened the reins.

"Giddy-up," she commanded. Doodlebug walked slowly, perfectly, once around the corral, then he looked over his shoulder at Jennifer. Well, she thought, we're off to a good start! She slapped the reins gently against the pony's rump. He broke into his beautiful flying trot, his long silky mane and tail streaming and all the metal parts of his harness jingling merrily. He circled the corral gaily, obediently, the cart following smoothly behind him. Jennifer's mouth dropped open. This pony must have already been trained!

She turned him, backed him, trotted him, walked him, all without a bit of trouble. It was plain that he enjoyed pulling the little cart. Finally she opened the corral gate and drove Doodlebug over to the barn where her father was turning the compost heap.

"I'll be darned!" he exclaimed when Jennifer showed him all that Doodlebug knew how to do. "Looks like you two are ready to go out into the world," he added, smiling.

So Jennifer began her goat milk and strawberry route. She was proud of Doodlebug and loved him through and through, but her face still got red when Myra trotted past them on the road with a superior smile that clearly said "*poor* little Jennifer and her *poor* little pony" or worse yet, something that sounded like a compliment but was really an insult. Like the time she stopped and pretended to admire Doodlebug, then said, "That little Doodlebug is the sweetest little workhorse I ever saw!" Jennifer just about exploded.

"Well, he's a lot more useful than Daisy," she

gritted. "Daisy doesn't do anything to earn her keep. She just eats grass."

"Daisy doesn't *have* to work for a living," Myra replied loftily. "My allowance is big enough to take care of both of us. And besides, you can't even ride your dumb pony, even if you want to, while Daisy has about the smoothest trot in the world." And with that, Myra wheeled the mare around and trotted off down the road. It was indeed a very smooth trot.

Jennifer choked back angry tears and clucked to Doodlebug to start pulling the little cart again. There was goat milk to be delivered before it got sour in the warm morning sunshine.

Jennifer might have been jealous of Myra forever if something hadn't happened to change everything in one short moment.

It happened one Saturday morning when Jennifer was coming home over the hill and met Myra riding Daisy, stuck-up as ever. Just then a big car passed them both and then screeched to a halt a few yards down the road.

Jennifer pulled the high-stepping Doodlebug to a quick stop and Myra turned Daisy to see what was going on. A man and a woman jumped out and ran back to the pony cart. The man took hold of Doodlebug's reins and the woman looked into Doodlebug's ear and nodded as though Jennifer weren't even there. Then they both turned to the girl in the cart and exclaimed almost together, "Where did you get Doodlebug!"

As Doodlebug was whickering a surprised welcome at the strangers, Jennifer sat up straight with amazement. Doodlebug was *never* that friendly with people he didn't know!

"Who are you?" she squeaked. Myra had dismounted and was watching curiously.

"Someone stole Doodlebug from his paddock last winter," the woman explained excitedly.

"But I bought him at the auction with my own money!" Jennifer objected hotly. She climbed down out of the cart shakily and stood between Doodlebug and the man and woman.

"You bought him?" asked the man, frowning.

"Yes, I did! The butcher wanted to buy him and I only had fourteen dollars that I'd saved for a Beautiful Black Stallion but I just had to buy Doodlebug because he was hurt and I doctored him and soaked his leg and walked him and brushed him and . . . and . . ." Jennifer gulped, trying to swallow the lump in her throat. "He's mine and I love him. Even if he *is* only a cart horse!" Jennifer's eyes were full of tears as she stroked the shiny black coat gently. The man reached down and picked up Doodlebug's lame leg.

"He was once a champion," the man said softly. "We saw that he had a slight limp as we passed, but we knew in a second that it was our Doodlebug." He felt the leg carefully. "He'll never win first prize pulling a sulky in the ring again," he finished sadly.

"The ring?" echoed Jennifer, puzzled. "Pulling a sulky?"

"Doodlebug is a registered Hackney Pony," the woman explained, smiling. "His fillies and colts are famous all over the country. We never thought we'd see him again." She stroked Doodlebug's nose.

Jennifer couldn't help it — she started to sob. They were going to take Doodlebug away. She felt as if someone had given her something wonderful then snatched it back.

"You actually mean," Myra snorted, "that dumb pony is *valuable?*"

The man smiled down at her. "Well, he's probably worth about fifteen pretty mares like that one of yours. She's a very nice horse," he added quickly, not wanting to hurt Myra's feelings.

Myra bit her lip and looked sideways at Doodlebug. Suddenly Doodlebug didn't look like a cart horse anymore. Her face turned red with embarrassment. Sheepishly she mounted Daisy and rode away. Jennifer was so upset that she didn't even notice when Myra left.

The man and woman walked a few yards up the road and talked quietly while Jennifer climbed miserably into the little cart, wishing she could trot little Doodlebug back into the past where he had belonged only to her. Soon they walked back to Jennifer.

"Honey, where do you live?" asked the woman.

"Just down the hill." Jennifer could hardly see through the tears. She pointed in the direction of the farm.

"Why don't we go to your house and talk about Doodlebug?" the man suggested. So they did, the expensive car slowly following the bright cart.

At the farm house they sat around the kitchen table with Dad drawing circles on the oilcloth with his finger and Mom sipping her coffee thoughtfully. The man and woman, who were called Mr. and Mrs. Daniels, discussed their plan while Jennifer looked through her tears from one to the other trying to understand. And suddenly she began to realize what the Daniels were telling her.

"Of course," Mr. Daniels was saying, "Doodlebug can never win in a show ring with that limp, so his show days are over. We can't tell you how grateful we are for your taking Doodlebug in and spending so many hours and so much care to heal him as well as you did."

"He's happy here, that's easy to see," said Mrs. Daniels. "And you take as good care of him as we could at our stables, and he certainly gets more love and attention than we could ever give him with our

eighteen other ponies to take care of."

"So if you'd like to keep Doodlebug here . . ." Mrs. Daniels started to say, but she couldn't finish the sentence because Jennifer had leaped from her chair and was hugging her with delight.

"Oh, *would* I!" Jennifer gasped. Then she hugged Mr. Daniels, too, and in a whirlwind of joy she finished up with a giant hug for her mom and dad together while the Daniels smiled at each other quietly.

Jennifer could hardly hold all her happiness as she listened to the rest of the arrangement.

The Daniels would bring mares to the Dickens' pasture to visit Doodlebug, and the little black Hackney Pony stallion would breed little champion colts and fillies just as he once had done in his paddock on the Daniels' Pony Farm. And the Daniels would pay for his hay and grain, and best of all, they promised to bring Doodlebug's own sulky for Jennifer to use.

Her parents and the Daniels were so deep in discussion that no one noticed when she slipped away to the pasture. And there, with her cheek pressed to Doodlebug's black velvet nose she whispered, "Hey, Doodlebug, you can stay here with me!" She leaned back in the grass and grinned at him as he reached over to nibble at her braid.

"How come I never guessed that my very own Beautiful Black Stallion with Flowing Mane and Tail was right here under my nose all the time?"

And the little black stallion whuffled contentedly.